In the front yard of a little house,
on the branches of a mighty evergreen,
there lived a happy pair of cardinals.

Red & Lulu

MATT TAVARES　　　　*Candlewick Press*

Red and Lulu were happy in their tree.

Their nests were always safe in its branches.
Its shade kept them cool on hot summer days.
And its evergreen needles kept them cozy
when autumn winds howled.
It was the perfect place to live, all year long.

But their favorite time of year, by far, was winter.
The family would decorate the tree with lights,
and sometimes people would gather near and sing:

O Christmas tree, O Christmas tree,
Thy leaves are so unchanging. . . .

Red and Lulu loved listening
to the people sing about their tree.
Sometimes they even sang along.

One chilly morning, just as the cold months were starting again,
Red went out to find some breakfast.
Lulu stayed behind,
tucked in the branches of their tree.

When Red returned,
he could not believe
what he saw.

Their tree had moved!
It was on its side, strapped to the back of a big truck.
Red could hear the sweet sound of Lulu's song,
coming from inside the tree.
And then the truck drove away.

Red chirped frantically, telling Lulu to stay right where she was,

telling her that he would be right there.

Red flew as hard as he could for as long as he could,
but the truck was just too fast.
Before long, Red lost sight of the tree.

Still, he kept flying, trying to catch up.
Soon he found himself in a strange place,
unlike any place he had ever seen.

For days, Red searched everywhere.
He was tired. And hungry.
He wondered if he would ever see Lulu again.

The snow reminded him of Lulu. He missed her so much,
he could almost hear the song they loved:

O Christmas tree, O Christmas tree,
Thy leaves are so unchanging. . . .

Wait! He *could* hear the song they loved! Red flew toward the sound.
The voices grew louder and louder.
Then he turned the corner.

Red chirped with glee and
soared over the singing crowd.

He flew right for their favorite branch.

Lulu!

Red and Lulu were happy in their tree
and watched with pride as hundreds of thousands of people
marveled at its beauty.

But then one day,
workers came and took their tree away again.

This time, Red and Lulu stayed.

They found a new place to make a home,
in a park surrounded by trees
and grass and lots of friends.

Now every year, when the air turns cold,
Red and Lulu take a special trip.
And when the crowd comes to sing, they sit together,
snuggled close on a snowy branch, and listen.

O Christmas tree, O Christmas tree,
Thy leaves are so unchanging. . . .

Sometimes they even sing along.

The Rockefeller Center Christmas Tree

Before there were even any buildings in New York City's Rockefeller Center, there was a tree. On Christmas Eve in 1931, construction workers decorated a twenty-foot evergreen with whatever they could find — strings of cranberries, paper garlands, tin cans, and even foil gum wrappers. Little did they know that they were starting a tradition that would last for eight decades and beyond.

Now every year, the head gardener at Rockefeller Center searches far and wide for the perfect Christmas tree. The chosen tree is almost always a Norway spruce, a type of tree that is not native to the United States. So it's usually found not in the forest but in someone's yard, where it was planted decades ago.

Once on its pedestal, the Rockefeller Center Christmas tree stands as tall as an eight-story building and is decorated with more than 45,000 multicolored lights. The star on top weighs 550 pounds. Every year on the first Wednesday after Thanksgiving, 200,000 people pack into Rockefeller Center to watch the annual tree-lighting ceremony, while millions more watch on television. And every day until the tree is taken down in January, hundreds of thousands of people visit Rockefeller Center to see the world's most famous tree.

When the holiday season is over, the Rockefeller Center Christmas tree is donated to Habitat for Humanity, a charitable organization that uses lumber from the tree to build homes for families in need.

Acknowledgments

Thanks to the pair of cardinals who visited my backyard countless times, finally convincing me to write a story about them. And thanks to my agent, Rosemary Stimola, who told me about the time her family was decorating their Christmas tree, only to find a certain winged stowaway hiding in its branches. Thanks to my family and friends who read this story in all its many versions over the past several years, kindly offering helpful feedback and encouragement, especially Manny and Jane Tavares; Sarah, Ava, and Molly Tavares; Ryan Higgins; and Aaron Becker. Thanks to Pam, Adian, Antwan, and Adian J. Green, who posed as the family who live in the little house. And special thanks to Katie Cunningham, Kristen Nobles, Hayley Parker, and everyone at Candlewick Press who helped bring this book to life.

The Empire State Building image ® is a registered trademark of ESRT Empire State Building, L.L.C., and is used with permission.

The New York Public Library image is used with permission from The New York Public Library.

First edition 2017

Library of Congress Catalog Card Number pending
ISBN 978-0-7636-7733-6

17 18 19 20 21 22 TLF 10 9 8 7 6 5 4 3 2 1

Printed in Dongguan, Guangdong, China

This book was typeset in Horley Old Style.
The illustrations were done in watercolor and gouache.

Candlewick Press
99 Dover Street
Somerville, Massachusetts 02144

visit us at www.candlewick.com

*For my friend Bob Sprankle,
who soared*